THE
HAPPY LION
ROARS

THE HAPPY LION ROARS

By **Louise Fatio**
Pictures by **Roger Duvoisin**

Alfred A. Knopf  New York

The Happy Lion was most unhappy, that was easy to see.
No one knew why, but there he was, refusing his food,
looking most of the time sadly up to the sky, sighing.

He looked sad even when he took children for a ride,
and yet, he loved those rides so.
When his friend François visited him, he no longer smiled and winked.
The doctor was called at last, but only said,
"A healthy young fellow, nothing wrong with him."
And he patted him on the head, left some pills, and went.
Yet, the Happy Lion was unhappy, that was certain.

"Ah," the Happy Lion would sigh to himself, "as I see every day, people and animals never seem to live alone, never.
The camel in his yard over there,
he rubs his head against Mrs. Camel's.
He is not alone.

"The hippopotamus, he splashes in the water
with Mrs. Hippopotamus and Little Hippopotamus.
He is not alone.

"The bear who wrestles playfully with Mrs. Bear,
he is not alone.

"The zebra, he rests his neck on Mrs. Zebra's.
He is not alone.
The gentlemen in town who come to see me with their ladies,
they are not alone.

"Even the tiny mouse comes to gather my crumbs
in company with Mrs. Mouse.
He is not alone.

"WHY AM I ALONE IN MY HOUSE?"

The Happy Lion was most unhappy, that was easy to see.

One day, a small circus (not Mr. Flambeau's)
came to town and set up its tent at one end of the park.
François and the Happy Lion went out to watch
the acrobats on the high wire, the bear who rode a bike,
and the jungle animals who sat on stools and roared.
But the Happy Lion saw nothing of these wonders.
He stopped in front of a red cage with gilded decorations,
and sat there all afternoon.

Why? . . . because . . . there lay in that cage,
with her paws crossed under her, kitten-fashion,
the most beautiful lioness in the world.
She had soft, green, sleepy eyes and a shiny yellow coat.
Oh, she was so beautiful. A real princess of a lioness.
When the Beautiful Lioness saw the Happy Lion,
she closed her eyes. No, not quite,
just so she could watch him through one tiny, tiny slit.
So the Happy Lion watched the Beautiful Lioness
and the Beautiful Lioness watched the Happy Lion.

And when François came out of the circus tent,
the Beautiful Lioness was still watching the Happy Lion
and the Happy Lion was still watching the Beautiful Lioness.
Indeed, François could not make the Happy Lion come home.
He called him,
he pulled him,

he pushed him.
The Happy Lion would not budge.
When the Happy Lion finally got up and left, with many sighs,
François could not tell whether they were happy sighs
or more unhappy ones.

The next day, François and the Happy Lion went to the circus again,
and while François watched the ring,
the Happy Lion watched the Beautiful Lioness.
What he said to her no one heard, I guess.

It is only certain that he sighed no more that night.
As soon as the gay moon was up in the sky,
he slipped out of his house, for now he knew how to open doors,
and he went silently across the darkened park
toward the circus tent and wagons.

The Beautiful Lioness was surely waiting for him,
for, when he opened the door of her cage,
she jumped down and followed him.
Together, they walked back through the park,

treading softly so as not to wake up
the noisy jungle birds and the cageful of monkeys.
The Happy Lion led the Beautiful Lioness into his house
and hid her way back in his cave.

When Monsieur Trapeze, the circus man, saw
that his Beautiful Lioness had run away,
he pulled his red hair in despair
and then called Monsieur le Maire and the policemen.
And then everyone who had nothing better to do
came to help in the search for the Beautiful Lioness.

Everyone looked everywhere a Beautiful Lioness could hide.
In the woods,
under old stairs,

in cellars and dark alleys,
behind woodpiles, and even under beds.

But there was no Beautiful Lioness.
Then they even went to look in the jungle-bird cage,

in the elephant's yard, in the hippopotamus' yard,
and, why, yes . . . even in the Happy Lion's house.

But what did they find in the Lion's house?
Oh, just the Happy Lion sitting in front of his cave,
so peacefully, so innocently,
just as if he knew nothing about anything.

"No Beautiful Lioness here," said Monsieur le Maire.

"No Beautiful Lioness," said Monsieur Trapeze.

"No Beautiful Lioness," echoed everybody else.

So, they were about to give up the hunt when,
WHEN . . . a little girl cried,
"Oh, LOOK! The Happy Lion has two tails!"
That was true . . . so he had.

As he was sitting there in front of his cave,
he had one tail on his left, a tufted one, and on his right,
a sleek, smooth tail that swished elegantly, like a cat's.
"It's my Beautiful Lioness' tail," cried Monsieur Trapeze.
Indeed, there was the Lioness' tail, and at the end of it
there was the Lioness crouching behind the Happy Lion.

Monsieur Trapeze rushed to the door of the Lion's house to fetch his Lioness, but he stopped short because the Happy Lion roared the biggest, loudest, longest roar he had ever roared in his life.

The Lion's house trembled, the old tree in the garden trembled,
Monsieur Trapeze trembled and looked at Monsieur le Maire,
who looked at the gendarmes in astonishment.

"Oh, please, Monsieur Trapeze," cried François,
"do not take the Beautiful Lioness away.
I know why the Happy Lion was unhappy. He was lonesome!"
"Leave my Beautiful Lioness here?" cried Monsieur Trapeze.
"My Lioness who can jump through a ring of fire? NEVER."

"Well," said François, "the Happy Lion won't let you take her."
Monsieur Trapeze, Monsieur le Maire, and the gendarmes
looked at each other again.
They were PERPLEXED, which means that they did not know
what to do.
But then Monsieur le Maire said, "Let me speak to my council,"
and he led Monsieur Trapeze away.
Everybody left too, also François, who was very pleased
that the Happy Lion could roar so loud.

When Monsieur le Maire had his council about him, he said,
"Messieurs, since our beloved Happy Lion is happy again,
all on account of the very Beautiful Lioness,
I propose that the Beautiful Lioness remain with him.
And I propose too that we pay Monsieur Trapeze what he needs
to buy himself another lioness
who can jump through rings of fire. *Voilà*, Messieurs."

So, Monsieur Trapeze took the money and went to look
for another lioness,
and the Happy Lion now shared his garden
with the most Beautiful Lioness in the world.
Never again did he sigh at the sky
or look sad when François visited him.
And the Beautiful Lioness also became François' friend.